COUGHDROP CALAMITY

Stage 12

Andersen Young Readers' Library

Hazel Townson

COUGHDROP CALAMITY

Illustrated by David McKee

Andersen Press · London

First published in 1998 by
Andersen Press Limited,
20 Vauxhall Bridge Road, London SW1V 2SA

The rights of Hazel Townson and David McKee to be
identified as the author and illustrator of this
work have been asserted by them in accordance with
the Copyright, Designs and Patents Act, 1988.

British Library Cataloguing in Publication Data available
ISBN 0 86264 834 3

Phototypeset by Intype London Ltd.
Printed and bound in Great Britain by
the Guernsey Press Company Ltd., Guernsey, Channel
Islands

Contents

*For the staff and pupils of Butterstile Primary
School, Prestwich*

Your library is precious – use it or lose it!

1

The World's Greatest Problem

'Atishoo!' Young Kip Slater gave an almighty sneeze.

'Don't tell me you've caught another cold!' sighed his friend Herbie Coswell. 'That's your fourth this winter and I'll bet you've just passed it on to me!'

'And me!' added Arthur Venger the inventor, who had just met the boys at the computer display in Stamford's store. Arthur had decided it was high time he joined the great world of technology, though he had more serious projects in mind than the computer games the boys were keen on.

'Atishooo!' Kip really exploded this time, to the disgust of several passers-by who scurried anxiously for shelter.

Herbie Coswell stared thoughtfully at Kip's red nose and watery eyes.

'It seems to me,' he declared at last, 'that one of the world's greatest unsolved problems is the common cold.'

Herbie was accustomed to making such pronouncements, for he was generally acknowledged to be a genius and folks now expected him to have grand opinions.

'The common cold,' he went on, 'creates more misery and more lost working days than all the other illnesses put together. It makes people mean, dozy and bad-tempered, wrecks friendships and leads to disastrous mistakes. I wouldn't be surprised if the people who invented such things as homework, boiled cabbage and the atomic bomb had really bad colds at the time.'

Gesturing grandly at the computers in front of him, he rattled on with growing enthusiasm: 'Here we are, faced with the

most stunning technology the human brain can devise, yet no scientist can scupper our snuffles. We can trawl the Internet, but we can't snare our sneezes. Now that's a great pity, for if anyone does come up with a cure there'll be a huge fortune waiting for 'em, besides the everlasting gratitude of humanity, you mark my words!'

'Cor!' grunted Kip.

Arthur Venger turned to Herbie with a sudden twinkle in his bright blue eyes.

'You're right! Why didn't we think of it before? Do you know, young Herbie, you've just started me on my most brilliant project ever?'

'Oh no!' Kip emitted a croaky groan at the prospect of another of Arthur's wild experiments. For 'A. Venger, the Avenger' believed himself to be a crusader destined to right the ills of civilisation, and once he got started on a new enthusiasm there was no stopping him. Already, in the space of a single year, Arthur had tried to cure liars, litter-droppers, hot-heads and misers, each with ever more disastrous consequences. So Kip could only fear the worst from this new endeavour. This included his own personal misery, since he and Herbie would be expected to help, as usual.

Herbie, however, was delighted.

'That's the stuff, Mr Venger! You could find a cure if anyone could. In fact, I wouldn't be surprised if you were already halfway there. Remember last time you had a cold? I couldn't help noticing that it cleared up much more quickly than usual. You were working at the time on your cure for toothache and the mixture you had on the boil was filling the room with peculiar fumes. Now, I know you didn't have much success with the toothache, but just suppose you went back and examined those ingredients more carefully? Maybe you'd just need to add another pinch of something here and there . . .'

'Herbie, you're a genius!' Arthur interrupted excitedly, but that was no news to Herbie Coswell.

2

Big Money

'I've done it! I've actually come up with a cure – an INSTANT cure! – for the common cold!' cried Arthur Venger ecstatically after twenty-four hours of non-stop labour. The little redhead was so excited that despite his weariness he was actually dancing round the room.

'It's permanent as well! Wipes out the virus for ever!'

Well, at least the first part of his claim appeared to be true, for Kip was persuaded to test the results, and after only a few sniffs of Arthur's incredible potion Kip's cold had

miraculously vanished. Headache, cough, sore throat, blocked sinuses and runny nose had all disappeared like magic. The delighted lad could hardly believe his luck.

'I feel as good as new!' he marvelled, plucking away the muffler his mother had wound so protectively round his throat and chest.

'You'll feel even better soon, for we'll be billionaires in no time!' Arthur cried, generously intending to share his good fortune with his loyal helpers. 'All those toffee-nosed lottery millionaires can jolly well eat their hearts out, for I'll be richer than any of them. I'll be able to charge whatever price I like for just one tiny bottle of this precious stuff! Oh, this is a dream come true, a life's ambition realised! I must be the happiest man on earth.'

'Well, let's not get too carried away just yet,' cautioned Herbie. 'We've still got to sell it, and the stuff doesn't even have a name.'

'Snifitoff!' cried Kip at once, flaunting the flair for words which his mother believed was a family trait (this being why she had called him Kipling in the first place).

'See off your cough with Snifitoff!' Kip sang in lilting tones that Rudyard would have been proud of.

'All right, that will do for the moment,' agreed Herbie grudgingly, wishing he'd thought of the name himself. 'Next we need some clever advertising. Leaflets, posters, TV and radio commercials, that sort of thing.'

Arthur's face fell. 'Advertising costs money. Big money. And until I sell this stuff I'm broke.'

'The bank will lend you some. That's what banks are for.'

'No, they won't. I borrowed for my last experiment and when it proved such a flop they said never again.'

Herbie the genius was undaunted. 'So! We'll start by offering free sniffs, just here in Grumpton. If we start at the bus station word will soon spread around. People will ring up their far-flung friends and relatives and before you know it, millions all over the

15

world will be clamouring for the stuff.'

'Herbie, you're . . . !'

'No need to keep reminding me!' retorted Herbie Coswell smugly.

3

A Laugh a Minute

It was one minute past nine a.m. as Tommy Mills closed the factory doors beneath the huge illuminated sign: KOPMAN'S COMICAL COUGH SWEETS – A JOKE ON EVERY WRAPPER! Any worker who wasn't in the building by this time would now have to ring the bell and find himself in big trouble.

Tommy was Foreman Joke-Writer and general timekeeper at this busy Grumpton factory. From his huge, untidy desk in the Joke Room Tommy had turned out thirty years'-worth of giggly wrappers and was

extremely proud that his stream of humour had never once dried up. Throughout the whole of his career no two cough sweets in any packet had ever revealed the same joke on their wrappers.

The secret, he always told his trainees, was to think jokes all day long and to try them out constantly on one's fellow workers. True to this tradition, Tommy would enter his office each morning with a new gem already bursting from his lips and today was no exception.

'Right, lads! How do you get down from an elephant?' he challenged, tossing his hat towards the hat stand.

'You don't; you get down from a duck,' replied Alfie, the youngest and brightest trainee. 'You can't use that joke, Tommy, it's older than a jumble-sale jumper.'

'All right then, why is tennis such a noisy game?'

As nobody replied this time, Tommy provided the answer himself: 'Because every player raises a racket.'

Nobody laughed; the joke fell completely flat.

Tommy was disgusted. 'TENNIS racket – get it? Don't you know what a tennis racket is, you ignorant lot?'

'You shouldn't have to explain your jokes,' muttered Alfie.

'Especially to folks with bad colds. They're dot in the bood,' added Sam Smart, Tommy's second-in-command, who was suffering from a nasty cold at that very moment.

Tommy sprang to his own defence.

'I've worked here for thirty years and been Joke Foreman for nearly twenty. If I don't know by this time what the public will laugh at, then I might as well retire.'

'Go od, thed!' Sam encouraged hopefully from the depths of a man-size tissue.

At that moment the owner of the factory, Bruno Kopman, appeared in the doorway of the Joke Room, looking anything but amused.

'You might all be retiring sooner than you

think,' he announced ominously. 'I've just discovered that dark forces are at work trying to put us out of business. It seems some fool of an inventor reckons he's developed a cure for the common cold and he's hawking it round the bus station. My car's gone in for service, so I was down there myself this morning and bumped right into him. He reckons it's a proper on-the-spot cure. Not the steady comfort of a nice, soothing packet of cough sweets with a few cheering jokes thrown in. Oh, no! We're threatened with a complete and instant remedy, quick as a finger-snap.'

Bruno dramatised his message with a nasty finger-snap of his own, right in Tommy's face.

'A proper cure? That's what they promised the overweight pig when they made him into bacon!' smirked Tommy, unable to help himself.

'You won't be joking, Tommy Mills, when I tell you he's claiming this cure's supposed to last for ever. One sniff and you're immune from colds for the rest of your days.'

'But that's impossible!' sneered young Alfie, whose mother had always assured him that a job at Kopman's Cough Sweets was a job for life.

'Nothing's impossible, including our fight-back,' retorted Bruno. 'I know things look bleak, but at least time may be on our side. Grumpton folks take a lot of convincing. They're hardly going to be swept off their sensible feet by one little middle-aged redhead and a couple of schoolboys.'

'Oh well, if that's all we're up against . . . !'

There were general sighs of relief. The matter didn't sound too serious after all. In fact, Bruno had probably got hold of the wrong end of the stick; he was a rare one for jumping to conclusions. Tommy decided to lighten the atmosphere a little.

'What did the schoolboy say to the red-headed teacher . . . ?' he began, until Bruno silenced him with a scowl.

'Look, this is deadly serious. I'm not having hallucinations as some of you seem to think. This stuff's called Snifitoff and it actually works; I've seen it with my own eyes. One woman tried it, right there in the Dumthorpe bus queue. She had a streaming cold and decided she'd nothing to lose. Believe it or not, her cold vanished like snow in a microwave. It was uncanny, I can tell you. Sent shivers right down my spine. If we let a thing like this take hold we'll be out of business in no time.'

Suddenly this was sobering stuff. Jobs were at stake. Homes, holidays, new suits and cup-tie tickets were at stake. Not another joke passed anyone's lips. It was plain that immediate action was needed. Young Alfie was all for rolling up his sleeves and rushing off to the bus station at once to tackle the villains face to face. He even armed himself with the leg of a broken chair which had been littering up the office for weeks.

But sniffly Sam Smart was not so sure. Violence wasn't going to solve anything, he claimed. Anyway, if they thought the thing through properly they would realise that even if they fought and won, they'd be cutting off their noses to spite their faces. Didn't they all suffer agonies of colds

24

umpteen times a year, just as he was doing at this very moment? Well, now was their chance to put a stop to all this misery. If it meant the end of cough sweets, so what? The factory could switch over to bulls' eyes or humbugs, or even sticks of Grumpton rock. Failing that, there were always other jobs. The Boiling Room mixers and stirrers could go and work in a glue factory, and the Joke Room staff could switch to Christmas cracker mottoes or gags for TV comics. You have to move with the times, adapt to a changing world.

'It could be the bakig of us all,' Sam concluded.

Bruno was furious.

'How DARE you suggest such a thing? Is this what you call loyalty? I've looked after you all these years, providing top rate wages, smart overalls and two free cough sweets a day whenever you have a cold, and how am I rewarded? Now, at the first sign of trouble, you turn traitor!'

Bruno was so upset he had to pause for

breath. He was shaking with rage and would have flopped into Tommy's revolving chair if he hadn't remembered it was faulty.

'As for bulls' eyes, humbugs and rock,' he continued with rising hysteria, 'how can any of you believe that Kopman's would sink so low? Why, Kopman's Comical Cough Sweets are known the world over. Armies march on them. Kings, presidents and newsreaders swear by them. Harley Street doctors recommend them. No fishing fleet or polar expedition ever sets sail without them . . .'

'Well,' interrupted Tommy, 'my motto is, if you can't beat 'em, join 'em, as the bully said when he glued two victims together.'

'You mean – go over to the enemy?' cried Alfie, dropping his chair-leg with the shock of it.

'Why not? If this stuff really works, we could put drops of it into our cough-sweet mixture and take a big share of the profits. Just think of it! – Kopman's Comical Cough Sweets would be a world-wide sensation in no time.'

'They're a world-wide sensation already!' snapped Bruno nastily. He flexed his fingers as though preparing to throttle someone as he added: 'Fetch this fellow to my office. I think it's time we had a chat.'

Tommy glowed. He reckoned his idea had caught on, which meant a pay rise in the offing.

'Leave him to me, Mr Kopman.'

Without further ado, Tommy grabbed his jacket and made off towards the bus station. Young Alfie would have followed, but Bruno told him to get on with his work; he wasn't paid for gallivanting.

4

A Dangerous Enemy

By the time Tommy set out to fetch him, Arthur Venger was beginning to lose patience. He and the boys had been hanging around that bus station since dawn, when the earliest workers' bus came in. They had decanted the first precious Snifitoff sample into an old disinfectant bottle which Arthur offered generously around. Yet in all that time they had won over only one volunteer sniffer, despite the fact that Kip and Herbie were wearing huge cardboard placards advertising their product.

BEAT YOUR COLD WITH SNIFITOFF

INSTANT CURE – LASTS A LIFETIME! TRY A FREE SNIFF NOW!

To Arthur's disgust they were either being ignored or laughed at. It seemed nobody but that one brave woman volunteer wanted to risk looking foolish by sampling their wares. To the cautious Grumptonians a cold-cure was as crazy an idea as selling guaranteed-to-win lottery tickets at tuppence each. Besides, it seemed downright dangerous to go around sniffing a mysterious bottle without knowing exactly what was in it.

To make matters worse everybody seemed to be late for work, leaping from buses and rushing away as if their lives depended on their speed. They scarcely even bothered to comment, except for one old dear who told her friend: 'Don't even look! I bet it's another disaster waiting to happen, like Mad Cow Disease.'

At last, just when Arthur was deciding to pack up for the day, the situation changed. Instead of rushing heedlessly away, one man actually came rushing towards the little

redhead, waving a greeting and elbowing travellers out of the way with great determination. As the man drew nearer Arthur was disappointed to see that he didn't have a cold. Never mind; perhaps he was seeking

help for a suffering relative? Herbie, less optimistic, guessed it was some bossy transport official about to chase them away.

They were both wrong, for it turned out to be Tommy Mills, wearing a beaming smile which Herbie thought was much too good to be true. Tommy took Arthur aside and spent some time chatting earnestly with him out of earshot of the boys. He then began to lead the little redhead away in the direction of Kopman's factory.

Arthur had perked up considerably and was now looking extremely pleased with himself. He assured any passers-by who might be interested that he'd be back again at the same time tomorrow. Then he turned to thank the boys, who had given up their precious half-term holiday to help him.

'Off you go now, have yourselves some fun, and meet me again at my bungalow at two o'clock,' he told them, his sly wink and thumbs-up sign seeming to indicate that he was on the verge of a major deal and would have some stupendous news by then.

'Well, that's a relief!' sighed Kip, thankfully discarding his placard. 'Somebody seems to have realised the possibilities at last. It was a pretty slow start, but we were bound to win through in the end.'

Herbie was not so sure. 'Didn't you notice who that was? It was Tommy Mills, Bruno Kopman's henchman, which makes me very suspicious. The last thing Bruno needs is a cure for the common cold. I wonder what they're up to?'

Kip was annoyed. 'Why do you always have to look on the black side?' he grumbled. 'If that's what comes of being a genius, then I'm jolly glad I'm not one.'

When Tommy and Arthur reached the factory Bruno was waiting for them, but he didn't look half as pleased as Tommy had expected. For Bruno had had time to think. If he put this Snifitoff into his cough sweets as Tommy had suggested, they would sell all right. They would do marvellously well for weeks. But if Arthur Venger was right, then

once everyone had eaten one sweet that would be the end of it. (One solitary sweet, mark you – not even a bagful!) After that there would be no more colds; no more demand. Not another cough sweet would be required until the end of time. One good season, then crash! The bottom would fall out of the cough-sweet business in a very big way.

In fact, Bruno had come to realise that Arthur Venger was a very dangerous enemy. Drastic measures were called for, and before the day was out both Arthur and his Snifitoff would have to be severely dealt with.

5

A Case for the Doctor

On the very stroke of two o'clock Kip and Herbie arrived at Arthur's bungalow eager to hear his news, but it did not take them long to realise that Arthur was not there.

They waited patiently for a while, then Herbie began frowning anxiously at his watch.

'He should have been here by now. Something's wrong; I feel it in my bones.'

'He's probably celebrating,' Kip argued huffily. Why did Herbie always have to be so pessimistic?

Suddenly they heard the bungalow telephone ringing.

'I bet that's him trying to reach us,' cried Herbie. 'He knows we'll be waiting for him here as arranged.'

Without further ado he fished out the spare key from its hiding-place in the hollow under the back doorstep.

Herbie was right as usual; it was Arthur himself, pleading urgently for help.

'Thank goodness I've caught you! They've locked me up. I'm a prisoner in here and you've got to rescue me, Herbie; I'm relying on you.'

'Just calm down, Mr Venger, and tell us where you are.'

'Bruno Kopman's factory. I'm locked in the Joke Room on the first floor, and it's no joke, believe me. They've left Sam Smart outside the door to keep guard. Kopman's gone to hire a van with a loud-hailer. He says he won't let me out until I promise to drive round Grumpton in that van, announcing that the Snifitoff isn't safe and nobody must use it ever again. They thought they were being clever, disconnecting their phone so I couldn't get in touch, but luckily they didn't notice I was carrying my mobile. Hurry up and get me out of here before Kopman comes back!'

'Don't worry, we're already on our way.'

Herbie grabbed Kip by the arm and dragged him quickly down the garden, explaining the situation as he went. Unfortunately, they didn't get far. By the time they reached the gate a huge, expensive limousine had pulled up beside it and a man was leaning out of the driver's window, beckoning urgently to the boys.

Kip thought he had never seen such a smartly-dressed man in Grumpton, not even during the last royal visit. He must be someone pretty important.

'I'm looking for Mr Arthur Venger,' the man explained, glancing up from his street-map. 'I believe this is where he lives.'

'He's not in,' Herbie snapped, anxious only to get on with the rescue.

'Now, that's a pity because I've come a

long way especially to see him. I'm bringing important news, something to his advantage. In fact, since you are obviously his friends, you may as well know that I'm hoping to make him a very tempting offer connected with his latest invention.'

'Sorry, but you'll have to come back later.'

'I don't think you realise how important this is, young man! You must be familiar with Mr Venger's movements since you've just come out of his house (unless you are burglars, of course) so you should be able to tell me where he is.'

'Who are you?' demanded Herbie, indignant at being taken for a burglar.

'My name is Doctor Yess.' The man produced a gold-edged business card and thrust it towards the boys. 'Doctor Ambrose Yess of Harley Street. I specialise in ailments of the upper respiratory tract.'

('The breathing bits,' Herbie explained impatiently to a puzzled-looking Kip.)

'One of my former patients rang me up to tell me about this new Snifitoff product,

and I'm genuinely interested, though I haven't much time to spare.'

'Unfortunately, neither have we,' retorted Herbie, pushing the card into his pocket for future reference. 'But we'll pass on your message and Mr Venger will no doubt be in touch.'

He turned to go, but Kip grabbed his arm and held him back. The Kopman possibilities might have ended in disaster, but here, reasoned Kip, was an even better opportunity: a top-class doctor who would have no trouble selling the Snifitoff to his wealthy patients. Why, those patients might even include the royal family!

The doctor could see that Kip was wavering so he added slyly: 'You wouldn't want your friend to miss out on a deal worth at least half a million pounds, would you? I doubt if he'd thank you for that.'

Half a million! Wow!

Before Herbie could stop him, Kip had blurted out the truth, that Arthur was imprisoned on the first floor of Kopman's factory and they were just about to go and rescue him.

'Wise lad! Now you've got yourself some help, for we can rescue him together. Six arms are better than four. Jump in!' The doctor was already opening his car door for the boys.

'Sorry! We never take lifts from strangers,' explained Herbie firmly. 'A person of your standing should know better than to invite us.'

'Yes, of course; very sensible!' The doctor closed the door again with a somewhat bad-tempered slam. 'In that case I'll save you the trouble and rescue him myself. I know where Kopman's factory is; you'd have to be blind to miss it with that great, tasteless sign lit up like a Christmas tree.'

The car window slid to a close. Then as suddenly as it had appeared the car moved powerfully off again, turning neatly at the end of the road and heading back towards the factory.

Herbie glared at Kip. 'Couldn't keep quiet, could you? Had to let the cat out of the bag. Well, come on! We'll take the short cut across the fields and find out what this bloke's really up to. Right now I wouldn't even trust him with a bag of dolly mixtures.'

'But his printed card . . .'

'Anyone can have a card printed. Use your

brains and save your breath.'

They ran at the double all the way to the factory, yet despite the short cut they were obviously too late. The first thing they spotted was the ladder which had been propped up against the first floor Joke Room window. Then they saw the doctor's car speeding away from the town with Arthur Venger on the front passenger seat.

6

Beyond a Joke

'Now see what you've done!' Herbie rounded angrily on his friend. 'Why can't you ever keep your mouth shut?'

'What, and let Mr Venger miss out on half a million pounds?'

'When will you learn not to believe everything you hear? Honestly, Kip, you're the most gullible person I've ever come across.'

'Doctors don't tell lies.'

'Always supposing he *is* a doctor. Anyway, what about the one who told your grandad he was allergic to cauliflower when he'd actually got Shingles?'

'Well, you can't deny the general public is being pretty slow to catch on and we can't spend our lives going round all the bus stations in the country. So Mr Venger's going to need a sponsor, somebody who can market the stuff properly for him.'

Kip was so busy trying to justify himself that he didn't hear the approaching footsteps. He was taken completely aback when he and Herbie were both grabbed by the shoulders from behind.

'So!' cried Bruno Kopman. 'You two have been helping my prisoner to escape! Well, I think you'll be sorry because now I'm going to have to keep you as hostages instead, until your precious Mr Venger agrees to my terms.'

'It wasn't us!' protested Kip. 'We've only just arrived, and you've no right to keep us here against our will.'

'You won't get away with it,' Herbie added confidently. 'When we don't turn up at supper time our dads will tell the police. They'll start a massive search of every

building in Grumpton and when they find us here you'll probably finish up in prison.'

Bruno gave a cunning smile.

'I rather think this whole business will be settled long before supper time. Venger must have a mobile phone since he's told you where to find him. So all you have to do is to write down his number and I'll ring him straight away. He'll soon come back when he finds out I'm holding you two.'

By this time Tommy Mills had appeared on the scene and was removing the ladder by which Arthur had escaped.

Bruno hustled the boys into the factory, and before they could protest any further they found themselves in the very Joke Room in which Mr Venger had been imprisoned.

'You needn't think there will be any chance of escape this time,' Bruno warned them, 'because Mr Mills will be right outside that window keeping a wary eye on you. And he'll do a much better job than Sam Smart who was supposed to be watching Venger.'

Kip felt decidedly shaky. What a mess they'd got themselves into! The only way out of it seemed to be to write down Mr Venger's mobile number for Bruno, which Kip did.

'Good lad!' Bruno gave Kip a fatherly pat on the shoulder. Then, after checking that the window was now securely fastened, Bruno left the room and locked the door behind him.

'Great!' sneered Herbie in utter disgust. 'You've been a fantastic help, you have!'

'As a matter of fact, I have!' insisted Kip. 'Whatever you may think, it's best if Kopman does make that phone call so that Mr Venger knows what's going on. Otherwise we could be stuck in here for ever. And in case you hadn't noticed, this isn't all my fault. You were raring to rush round here before that doctor ever turned up, and we'd still have been caught, even if we'd managed to rescue Mr Venger, which I doubt. Anyway, it's no use quarrelling. We should be putting our heads together to think what to do. If we can get out of here before Mr Venger comes back we can warn him off.'

'Yeah, I suppose you're right,' sighed Herbie reluctantly. 'We ought to start searching. Maybe there's something right here in this room that could help us. Keys, or a tool we could use to force the lock. Let's look everywhere, leave no paper unturned.'

Kip was only too glad of the truce, so he joined in the search with a will. On the Joke Room desk there was a metal tray containing a huge pile of papers. Kip began riffling through them until something caught his eye. He stopped riffling and began to read:

'Why is Prince Charles like a Post Office? – Because he's a royal male.'

'How did the worm catch Egyptian 'flu? – From his Mummy.'

'Who wrote a book called *Common Plants of Britain*? – Dan D. Lyon.'

'Hey, Herbie! I've found the so-called jokes, the ones they wrap the cough-drops in. You won't believe how corny they are. Just listen to this!'

He began to read aloud some of Tommy's weaker efforts, but Herbie was not in the mood.

'Stop messing about and find something really useful. Time's getting on. Try the desk drawers.'

'Just a minute!' Kip was reluctant to

abandon this fruitful fund of fun. He gathered up another handful of joke sheets – and suddenly saw, revealed beneath them, the bottle of Snifitoff and the precious sheet of paper containing Mr Venger's formula!

Maybe Arthur had left them behind on purpose so that the doctor could not steal them. Or perhaps he'd not had time to pick them up when he was snatched away so suddenly. He could even have forgotten them completely, considering how absent-minded he was.

Kip lifted the bottle from its nest of jokes and waved it around triumphantly,

'How about this for something useful?'

'Good grief! Is that the Snifitoff?' Herbie was peeved because Kip had been the one to find it. 'Well, just you be careful with it. So far it's the only bottle brewed, so it's unique.'

Herbie had scarcely finished this warning when the bottle slipped out of Kip's hand. Kip gave a cry of horror as the glass hit the edge of the metal tray and shattered noisily.

Immediately the Snifitoff began to spread itself in a pungent pool all over Arthur's formula and Tommy Mills's jokes.

Both boys stood in shocked silence, surveying the ruin of a million hopes and dreams. For with relentless speed, the Snifitoff was reducing every scrap of paper to brittle, unreadable shreds.

7

Kidnap and Car Crash

Meantime the doctor's limousine was purring its luxury way towards London.

'Where are you taking me?' demanded Arthur Venger. 'I'd a meeting arranged for two o'clock. I want to go home.'

'All in good time,' replied the doctor. 'There's an agreement to be reached first, as I already explained.'

'I thought this was a rescue, not a kidnap.'

'So it is – and a timely rescue at that, considering what you've told me of Kopman's plans. I think I've earned my partnership, and half a million pounds is not to be sneezed at, if you'll pardon the pun.'

'On the contrary,' retorted Arthur, 'my Snifitoff, properly marketed, could cough up billions every year.'

'Ah! But you can't market it, can you? You've got no money, no connections. I, on the other hand, know everyone worth knowing in the medical world and my file of patients reads like a royal garden party guest-list.'

Arthur smiled confidently. 'But I'm the one who has the formula, and where would your precious connections be without that?'

'All right then, I'll make it three-quarters of a million. Plus all that fame. You can put your name on the labels. Don't forget you'll be at the centre of a great enterprise,' persisted the doctor. 'You will be known, admired and practically worshipped throughout the world. That's worth a great deal, isn't it? Bruno Kopman just wants to ruin your chances, whereas I am being as helpful as I can.'

'Abducting me against my will? You call

that being helpful?'

Yess gave an exasperated sigh. 'I've done you a bigger favour than you realise. That villain Kopman could have dropped you into the vat and boiled you up with the next batch of cough sweets and nobody would have been any the wiser. Have you thought of *that*?'

Before Arthur could reply, his mobile phone began to ring. It was Bruno. Arthur listened in growing alarm, then cried: 'Stop the car! Kopman's got the boys. We have to go back at once.'

'Sorry!' smiled the doctor, shaking his head.

'STOP THE CAR!' yelled Arthur, wrestling frantically with his seat-belt.

'You'd better keep that belt on in case we have a nasty accident,' warned Yess, increasing the speed.

But Arthur was free of the belt now. He was utterly shocked that the doctor could leave two children to their fate, especially when he had just been talking about boiling

vats. Driven by desperation Arthur made a grab for the handbrake and steering wheel. The doctor elbowed him aside but Arthur pushed back, determined to try to stop the car. It was a dangerous moment.

Suddenly there was a terrifying screech. The car lurched sideways, then swerved wildly from the road and ended up in serious conflict with a tree. The frightful noise of its impact was followed by an even more frightful silence, broken only by a startled skylark rising from the hedge.

8

A Thousand Jokes

'I don't believe it!' wailed Tommy Mills. He had just entered the Joke Room to check up on his prisoners and had come face to face with the ruin of his joke pile. 'A whole two months' supply turned into useless crumbs! What am I going to do? I'll get the sack for sure.'

'Don't worry, Mr Mills,' Kip muttered guiltily, 'we'll help you write another lot of jokes, won't we, Herbie? We know thousands.'

'Can't you remember the ones you'd written?' grumbled Herbie, who thought

Tommy's brand of jokes a complete waste of time.

'No, I can't!' snapped Tommy. 'Can *you* remember the conversation you had at breakfast time three weeks last Sunday?'

'That's not a fair comparison.'

'Well, never mind arguing. You just sit down and write me some jokes, or else . . .!'

Tommy's unspecified threat hung in the air as Kip and Herbie took up the pens and paper Tommy threw at them. They had barely covered half a page each when Bruno Kopman returned.

'Venger hasn't turned up,' he grumbled. 'I can't understand it. He couldn't have gone far in this short time and I'd never have thought he was the sort to leave his young friends in the lurch.'

'So you did ring him?' Alert at once to new dangers, Herbie sat up with a jerk. 'In that case, I bet they've had an accident. You'd better go out and look.'

Bruno stared hard at Tommy and Tommy stared back. Each knew what the other was thinking, that if Arthur were dead it would solve the whole problem very neatly.

'I'll drive out and see if I can spot them,' Bruno decided. 'You keep an eye on things here, Tommy, and you may as well put in a bit of overtime on those jokes while you're at it.'

Little did Bruno realise how much overtime was going to be needed. Poor Tommy looked so devastated that Kip almost felt sorry for him.

Yet it seemed help was at hand. As soon as Bruno had gone Herbie announced that he had suddenly remembered a book he had at home, entitled *The Thousand Best Jokes of the Century* by Fanny Bizness.

'I could fetch it for you, Mr Mills, then you'd catch up in no time.'

'Kopman's jokes are supposed to be original. It's cheating, stealing jokes from books,' muttered Tommy half-heartedly.

'Not in an emergency, surely? Anyway, who's to know?' Herbie grinned.

Kip listened in amazement. He knew quite

well that the last thing Herbie Coswell would ever possess would be a joke book. Besides, how could Herbie think Tommy Mills would be foolish enough to let him out to fetch it? Yet that was exactly what Tommy did.

9

Sheer Bewilderment

Arthur Venger opened his eyes. He seemed to be part way up a tree, staring into its middle branches. No; that couldn't be right; he never climbed trees. He didn't have the figure for it.

He lay quite still for a minute or two, trying hard to remember how he came to be where he was. Gradually he began to realise that he was in a car – a somewhat battered car – and that there was a man asleep beside him. It was all very puzzling.

Slowly the feeling crept over him that he was in danger. The sleeping man was his enemy, though he couldn't think why. This conviction was so strong that Arthur decided he must escape from the car. This was easier thought than done, as the passenger door no longer seemed to fit. But he managed to force it open in the end, tumbling out on to the grass in a rather undignified heap.

Unfortunately, the grass sloped gently down towards a deep and dirty ditch, into which Arthur rolled helplessly to rest. After another bewildered pause he picked himself up and staggered towards the road. He ought to go home, but which way was home? For no particular reason he decided to turn left and began doddering unsteadily along the roadside.

He hadn't gone far when a sharp voice called to him to stop. 'Hey, you! Come back here! We've important decisions to make.'

Arthur looked round to see his no-longer-sleeping companion from the car, bearing menacingly down upon him, shaking a warlike fist in the air.

So the feeling of danger was real after all!

Arthur tried to break into a run, but his legs felt as if they were just coming last in a sack race. He had almost decided to surrender to his fate when fortunately a lorry driver spotted him, pulled up and offered him a lift as far as Brimbley village.

'Where you heading for, mate?' asked the lorry driver.

'Same place as you,' replied Arthur, whose mind was still in a state of confusion. He was just beginning to realise that he hadn't a clue where he lived. Still, anywhere would do for the moment; he was only too grateful to be leaving his mysterious enemy a good few miles behind.

At last the lorry driver reached his destination and Arthur climbed out. He found himself on Brimbley village green where he sat for a minute, dazed yet curiously unconcerned by his plight. He would find his way home eventually. All that mattered was that he was safe from his enemy.

After a rest, Arthur explored around. A signpost on the village green pointed the way to GRUMPTON 1 MILE.

Grumpton? Well, that was as good as anywhere. Arthur took the signpost's advice and
started walking the last mile home.

Herbie Coswell could scarcely believe his
luck. Tommy Mills had been so keen to lay
hands on the non-existent joke book that he
had practically pushed Herbie out of the
factory door. The boy genius had already
worked out his plan of action, which was to
find the nearest telephone box and ring his
dad for advice. His dad's office was not far
from here. Maybe Mr Coswell would then
jump in his car and rush to the rescue. Or
maybe he would decide to call in the police,
who were much more likely to believe him
than they were to believe Herbie, for Kip
and Herbie had shared one or two awkward
moments with the police force lately. Either
way, help would soon be forthcoming which
was all that mattered.

Herbie was not too familiar with the area
round Kopman's factory, which was on the

outskirts of Grumpton in the Brimbley direction. However, there was bound to be a telephone box close by. Yet before Herbie had gone far he heard a voice behind him, calling to him to stop. A scared glance told him it was one of Kopman's employees by the name of Sam Smart, so Herbie started running. He didn't even pause long enough to notice that Sam was waving a bottle in the air.

There was a telephone box ahead, but Herbie dared not stop now, in case Sam should catch him up. So he ran on, with ever-increasing speed, until he was sure at least that Sam had given up the chase. Only then, when Herbie stopped for breath, did he notice the figure of a plump, bedraggled little redhead walking unsteadily towards him.

'Mr Venger!' cried Herbie joyfully.

The bedraggled figure stopped walking and stared at Herbie.

'Do I know you?' he asked doubtfully.

Herbie's heart sank. Had Arthur lost his

memory? It was obvious from the state of Arthur's clothes that he must have been involved in some sort of accident.

'Please let him be all right!' prayed Herbie silently, for Arthur's memory of the wrecked formula was all they now had left.

10

Sam Loses His Bottle

Sam Smart and Bruno Kopman reached the Joke Room at almost the same time. Sam was definitely high, bouncing into the room with a beaming face and concealing something playfully behind his back. By contrast, Bruno looked thoroughly depressed.

Sam's cold had miraculously vanished, though the others were too preoccupied to notice. Tommy and Kip were still wrestling with the jokes, Tommy chewing his pen and Kip scribbling fast with great enjoyment. Bruno had flung himself into a chair where he sat brooding on the fact that Arthur

Venger seemed to have got the better of him.

'Well, haven't you noticed anything different about me?' Sam demanded impatiently.

Tommy gave him a half-hearted glance. 'You've washed your neck,' he suggested, 'and about time, too.'

'Try again.' Sam refused to take offence.

Suddenly Bruno cried: 'Hey, your cold's gone! You don't mean to say. . . ?'

'Yes I do!' With a theatrical flourish Sam produced a bottle from behind his back.

'The Snifitoff!' cried Bruno and Kip together.

'But there was only one bottle, and I broke it.' Kip sounded really confused.

'The one you broke was full of specially strong liquid paper-shredder which happened to look the same as the Snifitoff,' Sam explained. 'Clever, wasn't I? Now, what's it worth to you, Mr Kopman, if I tip the contents of this genuine bottle of Snifitoff down the sink? Then all your troubles would be over.'

'You can't do that!' yelled Kip, leaping up to make a grab for the bottle. Bruno pushed him back into his seat again.

'Go on, pour it! Get rid of it quick and I'll consider a modest rise in your wages,' Bruno promised.

Sam waved the bottle tantalisingly in the air. 'Double wages at least, and a hefty bonus every Christmas, Easter and Bonfire Night,' he amended, 'plus four weeks' extra holiday with pay and my own swivel-chair.'

'Give me that bottle!' Bruno advanced menacingly on Sam who side-stepped neatly away from the sink.

'Just think! One long glug and you're in the clear. On the other hand, if I were to sell this bottle back to Mr Venger . . .'

The taunting went on for some time, but in the end Bruno had to agree to Sam's terms in writing, with Tommy as witness. The minute this document was signed Sam uncorked the bottle and poured its entire contents down the sink. Kip gave a cry of

agony as he watched the last precious drops disappear, but there was nothing he could do.

Bruno, on the other hand, was delighted. Suddenly feeling full of goodwill, he told Kip there was no need to keep him there any longer. He could go, provided he promised not to tell where he had been.

Tommy caught Kip's sleeve. 'Hang about, Mr Kopman, the boy's just doing a little job for me.'

'What job? If it's private stuff you shouldn't be doing it here, and if it's work, you should be doing it yourself. Let the lad go.'

Bruno shepherded Kip to the Joke Room door, where he turned and had the last word: 'All's well that ends well, eh? But not for you, Sam Not-So-Smart; you're sacked!'

Kip shot out of that factory like a bonfire rocket. He was overjoyed to be free again but dared not think what Arthur Venger would say when he heard what had happened to the Snifitoff. The news must be broken gently. Still, it wasn't the end of the world. What Arthur had done once he could no doubt do again, even without the written formula.

Thus consoling himself, Kip started out for Herbie's house to get news of his friend. Yet as Kip turned the first corner Sam Smart caught up with him.

'Wait for me, laddie! I've something interesting to tell you.'

Sam delved into a deep pocket and brought out yet another bottle, identical to the one he had just emptied down the sink. Surely, he mocked, Kip had not thought anybody would be daft enough to throw away the chance of a lifetime? No fear! He, Sam Mega-Smart, had filled two replace-

ment bottles to make doubly sure of success. Now Sam had every intention of selling the real Snifitoff (the bottle in his hand) to the highest bidder.

'I daresay that will be our friend Doctor Yess, the chap who slipped me a fiver to turn a blind eye while he rescued the redhead. But of course you can let your Mr Venger know, and see how much he can offer. They might even start to bid against each other, which would be really good for business.' Sam gave a satisfied chuckle. 'Who wants to work at Kopman's crummy factory when there are fortunes to be made by not working at all?'

Kip was appalled at Sam's attitude, and deeply worried. How could they be sure this bottle was the real stuff? If Sam had made two copies, he might have made half a dozen.

'You'll have to trust me,' Sam smiled. 'But I'll tell you what I'll do. You find somebody with a cold and I'll let them have a free sniff.'

11

A Sneeze Too Many

Early next morning Arthur, Kip and Herbie began a council of war. How could they save the situation?

Arthur was feeling much better, but was still a good deal confused as a result of the bump in the car. He felt he would never be able to remember the Snifitoff formula without his written notes. So it was vital to recover the genuine bottle from Sam. Its contents could then be analysed and hopefully reproduced.

Kip thought straightforward burglary would be the best idea. One of them could lure Sam from home while the others broke in and snatched the bottle. But Herbie said they would be foolish to break the law. The best way to deal with a man like Sam Smart was by cunning.

'We need to make him think the Snifitoff is dangerous, just as Bruno was planning to do via that loud-hailer. Leave me alone for ten minutes and I'm sure I'll come up with something.'

Arthur put the kettle on, then he and Kip retired to the next room to drink hot chocolate and let Herbie think in peace. But the kettle had not even boiled when the genius had his brainwave. Joining his friends in great excitement, Herbie explained:

'This plan involves you, Kip, in a difficult acting role, but I know you can do it really well.' Herbie had decided flattery was the best way to gain Kip's co-operation. 'This is how it works. You, Kip, were the first to try the Snifitoff, so it stands to reason you must be the first to suffer terrifying side-effects.'

'What sort of side-effects?' Kip didn't seem

at all thrilled by this idea.

'It's all right; you won't be in any danger. You'll just look as though you are. A skin disease is the easiest to fake. We'll paint ghastly green spots all over you and pretend they're the result of the Snifitoff. We can even make some of them into nasty boils using blobs of green plasticine with yellow dots on top. We'll also paint black under your eyes and blue on your lips. You'll look really terrible and it will frighten Sam to death.'

(Me too! thought Kip.)

That, Herbie reasoned, was when they would tell Sam of the antidote Mr Venger had managed to make for this killer disease. They would offer to exchange it for the genuine Snifitoff bottle and how could he possibly refuse?

'Oh, it's all very well for you,' grumbled Kip. 'You and your wacky ideas. I'm going to look a right idiot. Anyway, it won't work because he'll soon spot the paint and plasticine. He's not that daft.'

'No, he won't. We'll make him keep his distance; tell him it's really catching. Besides, you'll be in a shady corner to start with.'

'Suppose I say I won't do it?'

But even Kip knew there was no danger of that. He couldn't let his friends down, or lose the chance of a fortune. Accordingly, that afternoon Kip took to the sofa in Arthur's bungalow and lay absolutely still, looking like a tailor's dummy doused in greengage jam.

'Groan a bit,' suggested Herbie. 'Clutch your stomach. Roll your eyes. Use your imagination.'

'If you're not satisfied why don't *you* give it a go? I'm sure you'd make a much better job of it.'

Herbie pointed out that he had the even more difficult role of persuading Sam to come and see Kip. In the end, though, Sam's anxiety got the better of him after Herbie's lurid descriptions. If he was in for a dose of this horror he had better find out what it

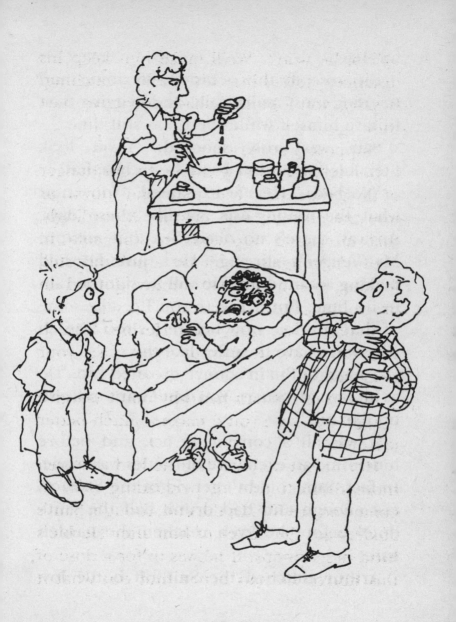

was like.

Kip rose to the occasion, moaning and writhing most realistically, and begging Sam to save himself while there was still time.

Sam was truly shocked. 'Y-you look t-terrible! Shouldn't you b-be in hospital?'

'No beds,' Herbie explained. 'You know what the waiting-lists are like these days. Anyway, there's no need. See that mixture Mr Venger's stirring? He's just finished making an antidote. Kip will be right as rain in no time. But if I were you I'd take some of that antidote now before it's too late, so you won't have to suffer like this.'

'Aaaargh! I'm in agony!' groaned Kip. 'Do as he says, Mr Smart. You don't want to finish up like me.'

It was all a convincing act, and before lunchtime an exchange of bottles was made. In fact, Sam couldn't get rid of the Snifitoff fast enough and had drunk half the 'antidote' before he even reached the garden gate.

Arthur clutched the Snifitoff bottle lovingly to his chest.

'My little beauty!' he crooned. 'You're going to make us rich after all.'

'Thanks mainly to me,' Kip pointed out, plucking sulkily at the huge blob of plasticine on the end of his nose. Surely Herbie needn't have gone to quite such lengths?

'I honestly didn't think we'd pull it off,' admitted Arthur. 'Fancy Sam believing all that rubbish.'

'He was up against a superior intellect,' smirked Herbie as the telephone began to ring.

It was Herbie's mother, explaining that a Mr Mills had just called at the house, claiming that Herbie had given him permission to borrow one of his books. The trouble was, Mrs Coswell could not find the book anywhere in the house.

'*Book of a Thousand Jokes,* he calls it. It's a new one on me.'

'Me, too!' grinned Herbie. 'Just a slight misunderstanding. You'd better tell Mr Mills the joke's on him.'

Herbie put down the phone and peered round the curtain to make sure Sam had really gone away.

'Hey! There's a taxi pulling up at the gate! It's that Doctor Yess.'

'You're never going to let him in?' cried Kip as Arthur moved towards the door. 'You can't have forgotten he tried to kidnap you?'

Arthur smiled. 'Oh, I think the doctor and I might be able to do business after all. On *my* terms this time. The scandal of that kidnapping is something I'm sure he would like to keep from his wealthy patients.'

Mr Venger actually had his hand on the doorknob when the disaster happened.

'Atishoo!' Kip Slater gave an almighty sneeze.

'Don't tell me you've caught *another* cold?' cried Herbie. 'That's your fifth this winter!'

Then, with dawning horror, he realised what that meant.

About the Author

Hazel Townson was born in Lancashire and brought up in the lovely Pendle Valley. An Arts graduate and Chartered Librarian, she began her writing career with *Punch* while still a student. Reviewing some children's books for *Punch* inspired her to write one herself. Fifty-four of her books have so far been published and she has written scripts for television. *The Secrets of Celia* won a 'best children's book' prize in Italy and *Trouble Doubled* was shortlisted for a prize in the North of England. She also chairs the selection panel of the Lancashire Children's Book of the Year Award. Hazel is a regular visitor to schools, libraries and colleges and her books have been described as 'fast-moving and funny'. She is widowed with one son, one daughter and four grandchildren.

The Speckled Panic
Hazel Townson
Illustrated by David McKee

When Kip Slater buys *truth*paste instead of
*tooth*paste, he and his friend Herbie soon realise
the sensational possibilities of the purchase.
They plan to feed the truthpaste disguised in a
cake to the guest of honour at their school
Speech Day but, unfortunately, the headmaster
eats the cake first . . .

'A genuinely amusing quick-moving story'
British Book News

ISBN 0 86264 828 9
£3.99 paperback (U.K. only)

The One-Day Millionaires
Hazel Townson
Illustrated by David McKee

Arthur Venger, inventor of the notorious
'Truthpaste', has a brilliant new scheme to
make everyone feel more generous. But when
villains cash in on his idea to make a fortune
for themselves, chaos ensues.

'A funny and fast-paced story for fluent readers'
Independent on Sunday

ISBN 0 86264 835 1
£3.99 paperback (U.K. only)

Trouble on the Train
A Lenny and Jake Adventure
Hazel Townson
Illustrated by David McKee

On a train trip to a Manchester museum, Lenny
overhears a sinister-sounding conversation. Has
he stumbled across a plot to blow up the train?
He tries to pass on a warning, but nobody will
believe him. So he and Jake take matters into
their own hands, ending up in a life-
threatening situation from which they have to
be rescued by a *girl*!

This is the fifteenth story in Hazel Townson's
popular *Lenny and Jake* series. The last story,
The Clue of the Missing Cuff-link, was praised by
the *Independent on Sunday* as a 'fast, funny and
hugely entertaining read'.

ISBN 0 86264 624 3
£4.99 paperback (U.K. only)

TROUBLE DOUBLED
including
Dads at the Double and Double Snatch
Hazel Townson

Two exciting mysteries by Hazel Townson are combined in this paperback original.

Dads at the Double
After meeting at a Schools Drama Festival, Paul and Sara, who live at opposite ends of the country, begin a correspondence. But their letters gradually uncover a horrifying truth which could devastate the lives of both families.

Double Snatch
Angela's weekend visits to her estranged detective dad involve her not only in his case-load but also in a frightening drama which puts her best friend's life at risk.

'The action is artfully advanced through correspondence'
Daily Telegraph

ISBN 0 86264 710 X
£3.99 paperback (U.K. only)